Dogs and Roses

BEGGS

£28.62.

NEWMAT

The Berridge Centre, Clarendon College, Nottingham.

Produced by NEWMAT — A Special Development Project
for Nottinghamshire County Council, funded by ALBSU.

British Library Cataloguing in Publication Data

Beggs, Karen, *1944* —
  Dogs and roses.
  1. English language — Readers — For slow
  reading adults
  I. Title   II. Beynon, Peter
  428.6'2

ISBN 1-871174-12-0

Printed by The Russell Press, Gamble Street,
Nottingham NG7 4ET.
First published 1988.

Dogs and Roses

CHAPTER ONE

Carol sat up suddenly in bed.

She looked at the clock on the bedside table.

She had a shock. It was almost 7.30 a.m.

''Come on kids!'' she yelled. ''Time for school.''

Anna and Mark jumped out of bed

and threw on their clothes without washing.

Carol put some bread under the grill to toast.

Skip, their Jack Russell dog,

ran round and round the kitchen table,

adding to the mess.

"Mark! Walk the dog," Carol yelled.

"Anna! Butter the toast, while I get ready."

The children started to fight as usual.

"It's not fair. I always have to take the dog out."

"No, you don't. I usually do it because you're always late."

"Not now kids, not now," thought Carol.

"Kids! Just try to get out of the house without fighting."

Mark went off with Skip.

They came back five minutes later.

The children each picked up a slice of toast.

They ran out of the front door into the High Street.

Carol gave Skip a drink.

She threw on her coat and followed the kids outside.

She raced across the road,

just in time to catch the 55 bus to town.

CHAPTER TWO

Carol sat at the back of the bus.
She thought about her life.
It was two years since Len had left.
Those two years had been hard and lonely.

Everyone said that she had coped well.
The kids were well dressed and looked cheerful.
They had been hard up.
She had worked as a cleaner, a child-minder and in a shop.
She had done almost anything to bring in more money
to add to what Len sent for the children.

Now she was on her way to a new job.
It was one she had really set her heart on.
She had been very lucky to get it.
A lot of people had wanted it, but the vet had picked her.

Carol loved animals and she needed a job.
She knew she would make a good assistant.
And she lived nearby —
she could be called if there was an emergency.

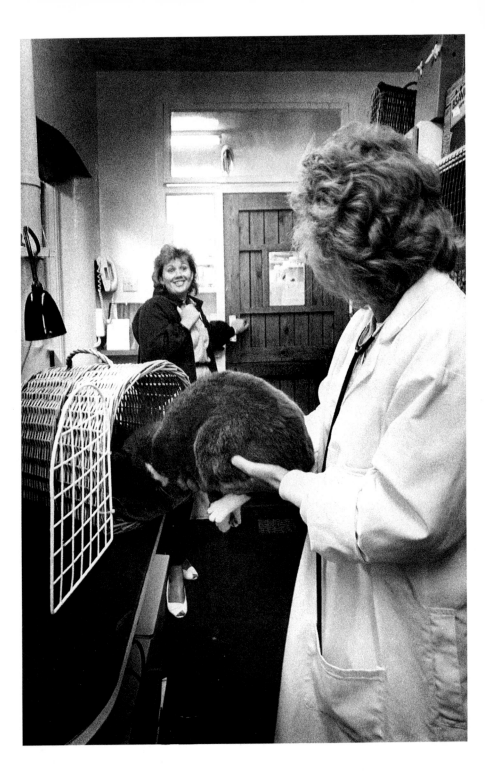

The green bus bumped along the busy streets,
on its way into town.
Carol got to her feet when she saw the vet's surgery.
She got off the bus and crossed the road.
She went into the surgery by the back door.

''Good morning, Mrs. Morris,'' the vet shouted to Carol.
''Good morning, Mrs. Young,'' said Carol.
The vet was pushing an unwilling cat
into a cane basket.
''Can I call you Carol?'' she asked.
''Yes, please do.''

''I'm going to enjoy this job,'' thought Carol,
as she opened the front door
for morning surgery.

CHAPTER THREE

Carol got back at 5.00 p.m.

She was pleased to see

that Mark and Anna had been cleaning the house.

There was a note for her on the kitchen table.

Dear Mum,
Done the kitchen and front room.
Gone to the park with Skip.
Hope you had a good day at work.
Love
Anna and Mark x x x

"Great," thought Carol,

"I'll have five minutes to myself

before I start making the tea."

She made a mug of strong coffee

and sat down in front of the T.V.

In no time at all she heard the kids at the front door.

Two hot and angry children burst into the room.

"Mum, Mum, guess what happened. . . . .
guess what happened in the park?
Look at poor Skip," said Anna.

Skip was covered with mud,
and he had a nasty glint in his eye.
Carol had seen that look before.
"He's been fighting, hasn't he?" said Carol.
"I've told you, he can't be trusted near other dogs.
You must keep him on the lead."

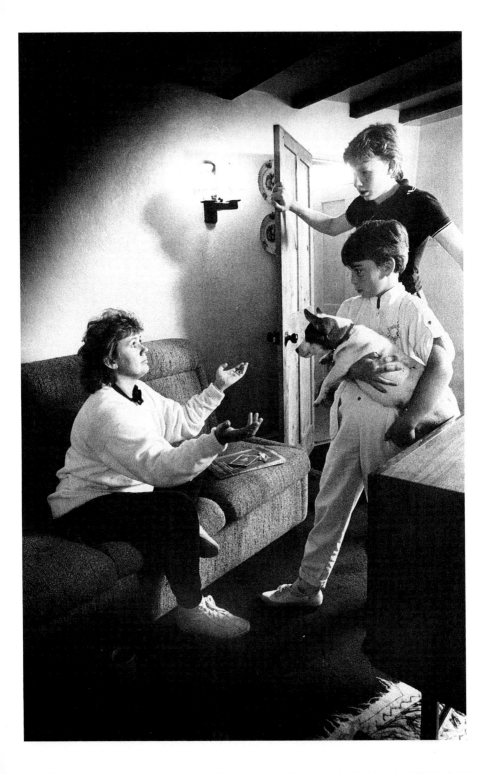

"But Mum," cried Anna,

"There was this old black and white Spaniel in the park.

Skip ran to see him.

And then they were fighting and rolling over in the mud.

We did try to stop them,

but this man came up and shouted at us.

He called us brats

and said that Skip should be put down.

He was really horrible."

"Never mind," said Carol,
"but next time keep Skip on the lead.
Was the other dog hurt?"
"Yes," said Anna.
"His eyelid was torn and his ear was bleeding."

Carol was upset.
She didn't like to think of any animal being hurt.

"Will Skip have to be put down, Mum?" said Mark.
"Of course not," she said. "Now let's clean Skip up.
We'll have some tea and forget about it."

One hour later everyone was fed and feeling happy.
They sat down in front of the fire
and Carol told the children
about her first day in her new job.

CHAPTER FOUR

The next morning was wet and cold.

Carol got to work in good time.

She opened the front door of the surgery.

Then she made coffee for Mrs. Young and herself.

''Thanks,'' said the vet. ''We have a lot to do today.

Can you feed the animals that we kept in overnight?

I'll start the surgery.''

There was a list of feeding instructions fixed to each cage.

Carol worked happily.

''First the cats, then the dogs.

Poor things, they do look sad without their owners.''

Then she spotted the black and white Spaniel.

It had a torn eyelid and a nasty rip on its ear.

''This must be the dog that Skip bit in the park'',

she thought.

There was a small card over the cage.

Name:	'Robbie' – Spaniel
Owner:	John Andrews
Address:	22 Spring Lane, Ashby.

"Hello Robbie," she said softly.
"Cheer up, you'll be going home soon."

Later that morning
a tall, good-looking man walked into the surgery.
Carol looked up.
He was about forty with blonde hair.
"I've come to pick up Robbie," he said.
"Oh yes — the black and white Spaniel.
Please come with me."

Carol led the way to Robbie's cage.

"Here he is," she said.

As soon as Robbie saw the man,

he wagged his tail and barked.

"He looks fine now," the tall man said.

"I've been quite upset about him —

he's old, you know."

He stopped speaking and patted Robbie.

"He was really my wife's dog.

She died just over a year ago.

She really loved him."

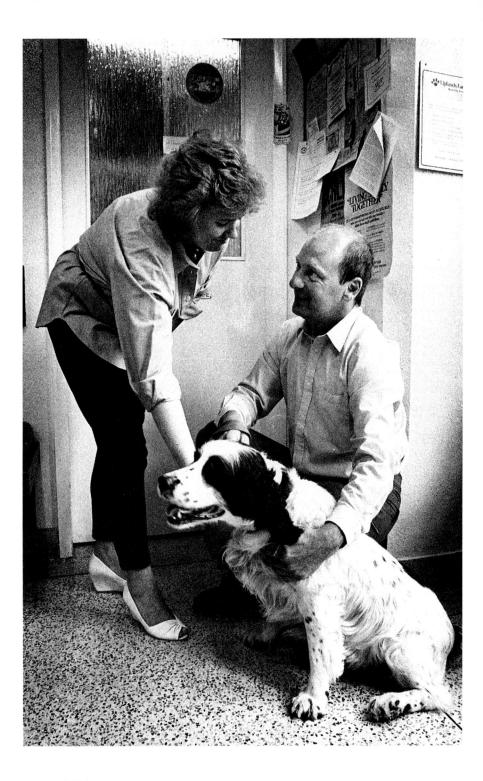

''Oh, I'm sorry,'' said Carol.

''I'm glad Skip didn't do too much harm,'' she thought.

Then she turned to John Andrews, and said,

''Don't worry! He's a strong old thing.

Come on boy, time to go home.''

Carol went with John and his dog to the door.

CHAPTER FIVE

Robbie stayed close to John
until they got to the lorry.
John opened the door.
The dog jumped in,
and licked John's face.
"Poor old boy,
you've had a bad time,"
said John, giving Robbie a hug.

John put the lorry into gear
and set off for his house.
He thought about Carol.
She was pretty — and kind.
He liked her.
Suddenly he felt very lonely.
"Never mind," he thought,
"Robbie will keep me company."

John often took Robbie with him in the lorry.
The dog loved to ride in the warm cab.
They went all over the country together.
Sometimes John went abroad
and Robbie had to stay behind.
This made him sad.

"We're off to Stoke this afternoon," said John.
"Then we'll go to Helen's for tea.
Is that O.K., old boy?"
Robbie barked.

Helen was John's only child.
She was twenty and had her own flat.
John had spent a lot of time with Helen
after his wife's death.
They had become very close.
But he knew that something was missing from his life.

CHAPTER SIX

Several weeks later,
Carol was coming home from work.
As she got near to the house,
she heard angry voices.

A man and a dog were standing by her front door.
Anna and Mark were just inside.
Skip was in Mark's arms.
''What's the matter?'' called Carol.
She was frightened.
The man turned round.
It was John Andrews,
with his dog by his side.

''Oh, it's you,'' she said.
''Are these **your** kids?'' he asked angrily.
''What if they are? Why are you shouting at them?''
John was shaking with rage.
''You need to teach them some manners
and as for that bloody dog of yours....''

"What are you talking about?" asked Carol.

"I was walking along the street with Robbie,
when your dog shot out and had **another** go at him.
And your kids were bloody rude.....
if I were their father, I'd give them a good hiding."

Carol's eyes filled with tears of anger and shame.
Her face was hot and red.
"Well, you're not their father,
and if you must know, he doesn't live with us."

"Oh," said John. "I didn't know."
Without saying another word, he left.

"What's been going on?" asked Carol, going inside.

"Anna was going to get an ice cream," said Mark.

"Yes, yes, and Skip got out," said Anna.

"It was an accident —
I didn't mean to let him out."

"And were you rude to that man?" asked Carol.

"He was rude to us," snapped Mark. "Bad tempered sod."

"Yes," said Anna, "he's a grumpy old...."

"That's enough," said Carol firmly.

She could see both sides of the story.
She was sorry for John,
but she was also sorry for the children.

"Alright, it was an accident," said Carol.

"But you must be more careful with Skip.

Now, let's get some tea."

Mark and Anna followed her into the kitchen.

They were still very worked up.

Carol felt very confused.

"He **seemed** such a kind man," she thought.

CHAPTER SEVEN

The kids were eating their fish-fingers,
when the door bell rang.
Carol went to the door.
It was John Andrews.
He was looking down at his shoes.
''Oh, no!'' thought Carol.
She couldn't face another row.
''I've come back to say I'm sorry,'' he said.
''Sorry to be so rude.
I didn't mean to shout at your kids.''

Carol felt better.

She was glad that John had come back.

He really was a kind man.

"I'm sorry too," she said.

"Skip is young and can be a bit daft.

The kids can be silly too!"

"No hard feelings?" said John.

"No," said Carol smiling.

"Good. So can I take you out for a drink on Thursday night?

I'll call round at 9.00.

By the way, I'm John."

"Yes, I know," she said,

but he'd gone before she had time to say any more.

She shut the door and went back to the kitchen.

The children were still eating.

"Who was that?" asked Mark.

"A friend," said Carol.

"We're going out for a drink tomorrow night."

She didn't know how she was going to tell the children

that 'the friend' was John.

One thing was sure —

they would not be pleased!

CHAPTER EIGHT

On Thursday evening Carol rushed home from work.
She gave the kids their tea
and had a bath.
She was feeling good
but a little nervous.
She hadn't been out with a man
since Len had left her.
"I must be mad," she thought as she got dressed.
"I don't know him very well."

At 9 o'clock she said goodnight to the children.

Carol stepped out into the cold night air.

She would wait outside.

She didn't want the children to see John.

She was still waiting at 9.15.

''He's very late,'' she thought crossly,

walking up and down the pavement.

By 9.30 Carol knew John wasn't coming.

She'd been stood up!

She let herself back into the house.

"Hi Mum, you were quick," said Anna.

"Did you have a good time?" asked Mark,
his eyes fixed on the T.V.

Carol sat down next to Mark on the settee.
She put her arm around him
and gave him a hug.

"They are good kids," she thought.
"I can always rely on them to cheer me up.
What a mean trick for John to play.
The pig! What a let down!
Men — they're all the same!
If I ever see him again, I'll...."

CHAPTER NINE

The next morning, as Carol was getting breakfast,
the door-bell rang.
Anna went to answer it.

She came back with a bunch of red roses!
''Hey Mum, look at this.
There's a card with it. Shall I read it?''
Without waiting, Anna began to read.

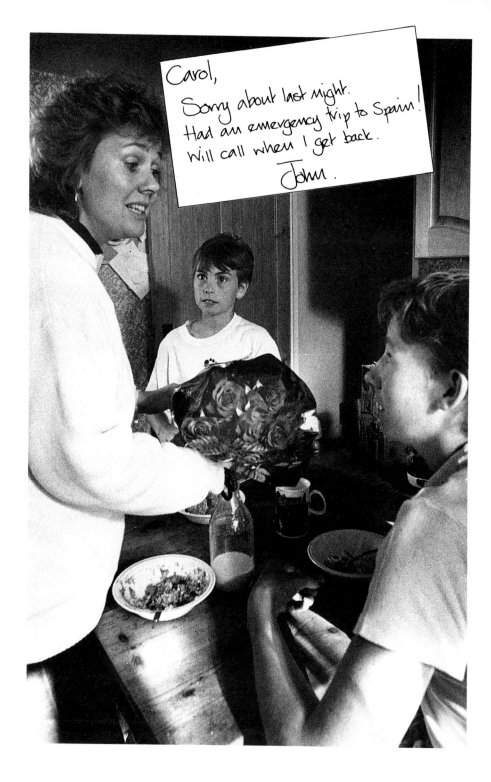

"Who's John?" asked Anna.

"Oh no," thought Carol, "I'll have to tell them."

"Um... he's the man with the dog —
the one Skip hurt."

"Oh Mum!" yelled Anna,
"You're not going out with **him,** are you?
He's horrible."

Marked gasped in surprise.

"I was only going out for a drink," said Carol.
"John was very sorry about the other day.
He's quite nice really. Look, aren't these flowers lovely!"
Carol found a tall white vase
and put the flowers in it.
"Now, it's time for school," she said.
The children left the house feeling upset.
Carol left for work feeling ten years younger.

CHAPTER TEN

Ten days went by,
and John hadn't called.
Carol was feeling low.
''Life can be so unkind,'' she thought.
Still, things are getting better.
I like my job.
Anna and Mark are getting on at school.
Money is not as short as it has been.
But — something's missing!''

That night,
as Carol was doing the ironing
the phone rang.
"Hello, this is John. I hope you're not angry with me.
I'm very sorry about the other night.
The trip to Spain took longer than I thought.
Can I still take you out for a drink?"
"What now?" said Carol. "It's ten o'clock!"
Her heart was beating fast.
"I'm in the phone box round the corner —
come on."
Carol thought for a moment —
"O.K., I'm on my way."

Carol ran into the bedroom.

She quickly brushed her hair and put on some make-up.

She ran downstairs.

Her heart was racing.

John was standing by the phone box.

He was smiling and he was very brown.

''Wow!'' thought Carol.

''Did you have a good trip?'' she asked.

''Not really. The lorry broke down in Madrid.

It took three days to get new parts.

But it gave me time to get you a present!''

He handed Carol a small packet.

She opened it.

Inside was a gold locket.

''Thank you. It's lovely.''

''And I bought some things for the kids,'' said John.

''I didn't want them to feel left out.''

''He is a kind man,'' thought Carol, ''I knew he was.''

They walked to 'The Windmill' and went inside.
It was warm and friendly.

John bought the drinks and they talked and talked.

Carol felt so relaxed.

So did John!

When the landlord called 'TIME',
John walked Carol home.

''By the way how's Robbie?'' she asked.

''He's alright, thanks.

He stayed with my daughter, Helen,

while I was in Spain.

If you like, I can pick you up from work

at lunch-time tomorrow.

We could take Robbie for a walk by the river.

Is one o'clock O.K.?''

''Great,'' said Carol. ''See you then.''

She let herself into the house,

feeling very happy.

CHAPTER ELEVEN

The next day, John picked Carol up from the vet's.
It was sunny and warm by the river.
John held her hand as they walked.
They both felt good.

Carol told John about her life with her husband.
She told him about the break-up and pain of their divorce.
She also told him about the good times
when Mark and Anna were small.

John told Carol about his wife.

She had died of cancer.

John had looked after her till the end.

They had been very happy and he missed her so much.

Helen had been a help, so had Robbie.

But he was still very lonely.

Carol wanted to stay with John,

but she had to get back to work.

"Thanks for coming today," said John.

"You know, I feel so good with you."

"Are you doing anything on Saturday?" he added.

"No," said Carol. "How about coming round for tea? It'll only be beans on toast!"

John laughed.

"I love beans on toast. I'll come round at 5.00. O.K.?"

"Yes, great," said Carol.

John smiled and kissed her cheek.

She waved as he drove off.

Carol felt like a teenager all over again.

CHAPTER TWELVE

On Friday night Carol walked into the house.

The phone was ringing.

She picked it up.

''Hi Carol, it's John.

I've just heard the weather forecast.

It's going to be fine tomorrow —

let's take the kids to Skegness.

I'd like to see you alone

but we've got to think of Mark and Anna.

I want them to like me.''

''That's a great idea,'' said Carol.

''I'll see you at ten. Bye.''

Then she thought about the children.

How would they take the news?

''Oh well, I'd better tell them now,'' she thought.

The children were in the kitchen.

''Listen kids, we're going to the seaside tomorrow.''

''Great!'' said Mark and Anna.

''John's taking us,'' Carol added.

''Oh no, he's not,'' shouted Mark.

''We hate him —

he's a right........''

''I don't want to go with **him**!'' cried Anna.

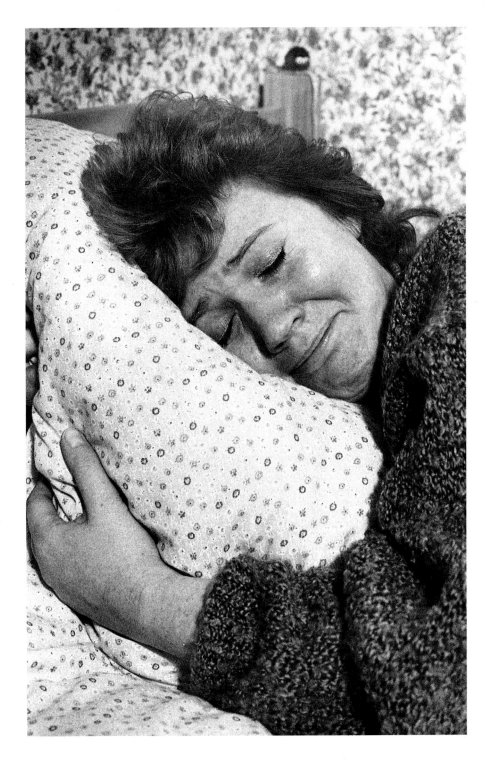

Mark was angry and his sister had tears in her eyes.

Carol was crying too —

she didn't want to upset the children.

She wanted them to be happy.

But she had to have some life of her own.

''Look kids, please give it a try.

It's hard for all of us.

I'm fond of John — he's a good man.

I need someone too.''

Carol went to her bedroom.

She lay on her bed and sobbed into the pillow.

Mark and Anna sat in the kitchen and sulked.
At last, Mark said to Anna,
"Poor Mum. We could have one day out with him
and see what happens.
But I hope Mum isn't going to make a fool of herself!"
"Alright," said Anna, "it could be fun at the sea-side.
But I'm only going if Skip comes too."

CHAPTER THIRTEEN

The sun was shining into the bedroom
when Carol woke on Saturday.
It was a great day for the trip.
She made a picnic and packed the swimming things.
The children were waiting in the hall with Skip.

John arrived on time.

He had brought a bunch of red roses for Carol
and two bags of sweets for the kids.

Mark and Anna looked happy.

So did Carol.

Then John saw Skip. His face fell.

"Oh.... I've got Robbie in the car," he said.

"Don't worry," said Carol.

"Skip can sit on my lap in the front."

She looked long and hard at John.

"Fine.... fine," he said, "Robbie in the back,
Skip in the front. No problem!"

John didn't sound very sure.

"What have I let myself in for?" he thought.

As they went out to John's car, Carol was thinking,
''What am I doing? I must be mad.
I am fond of John, but to go with him,
two kids and two dogs to the sea-side....''

John started the car.

He pulled out into the traffic.

He began to sing softly to himself —

''Somewhere over the rainbow,

Skies are blue....''

John smiled at Carol
and she smiled back.

The Cast

Carol Morris	*Sue Young*
Anna Morris	*Nancy Beggs*
Mark Morris	*Paul Housley*
John Andrews	*Terry Elston*
Mrs. Young, the Vet	*Karen Beggs*
Skip	*Toyah*
Robbie	*as himself*

Other NEWMAT Titles

'Rock Biographies'
Twelve titles about key figures in rock music.

David Bowie	Elvis Presley
Bob Dylan	The Rolling Stones
John Lennon	Diana Ross
Madonna	The Sex Pistols
Bob Marley	Tina Turner
The Police	U2

'Routeing Around Wales'
'Routeing Around The Heart of England'

Two guide books to the sights, history and industry
of places in the U.K. Illustrated, with photographs,
maps and diagrams.

'A Stab in the Heart'

A murder mystery story set in Los Angeles in 1940.

All titles available from:
Adult Literacy and Basic Skills Unit
Kingsbourne House, 229/231 High Holborn,
London WC1V 7DA
Telephone: 01-405 4017

With special thanks to....

Caroline Baker and Cathy Knowles,
for their help with the text.

Tim Ireland, for the use of his house.

Townley and Reeves, Veterinary Surgeons,
for the use of their premises.

Ivor and Dos Harwood
at 'The Three Crowns',
for the use of their premises.